THE
ISADORA INTERVIEWS

THE NETWORK SERIES
by Katie Cross

Miss Mabel's School for Girls
Antebellum Awakening

THE
ISADORA INTERVIEWS

Katie Cross

Antebellum
Publishing

The Isadora Interviews

Young Adult Fantasy

Text copyright ©2014 by Katie Cross

Cover designed by Jenny Zemanek, Seedlings Design Studio (www.seedlingsonline.com)
Typesetting by Atthis Arts LLC (www.atthisarts.com)

Published by Antebellum Publishing
www.antebellumpublishing.com

ISBN (paperback)   978-0-9915319-6-7
(ebook)   978-0-9915319-2-9

Visit the author at www.kcrosswriting.com

Visit The Network Series at www.missmabels.com or on
Facebook at www.facebook.com/missmabels

Leda

Leda opened the door of the closet just enough for one olive green eye to peer out. The other eye, the color of straw, closed so she could focus.

Rain trickled down the windowpane of her small bedroom, and she let out a content little sigh. Hibernating in the warm house when the earth crawled with cool mist was one of her favorite things. She leaned back into the closet with the quiet *snick* of the door closing.

Straightening her spine, she worked out the kinks in her back with a deep breath. Spending two hours stooped over a book in a closet barely big enough for her to lengthen her legs was less than ideal, but at least it was private, no easy feat in a family of eight children. With a pinch of her fingers, she extinguished the candle flame and shoved the books on potionmaking away from her.

Rosemary twigs. Pecan shells. Simmer on a blue flame. Moonlight for six hours.

An extraordinarily difficult potion sat on her mind and had for many days, percolating in the background of her thoughts. No one had ever gotten the Forgotten Potion right, which is exactly why Leda wanted to make it. It restored lost memories. Not like a generalized memory potion, either. It could bring back a specific, imperfect memory, rooting it out from childhood if necessary.

Maybe I could use it on myself and remember the wretched day I received this curse.

Leda pushed her white-blonde hair away from her face. There was really no use reviewing the Forgotten Potion any longer. She didn't have the time to try it, not with all the studying she had to do.

One day. One day I will try it.

By the time she extricated herself from the books and the tiny closet, her siblings' voices had moved from their bedrooms into the dining room. Mama's called out over them. The sound of her voice, and the meaty smell of stew in the air, meant dinner was just about to start. Dinner meant Papa would be home.

Motivated by the thought of Papa's return, Leda quickly slipped the scroll underneath the mattress with her stubby pencil, tucking them back as far as they could go. Anything that could rip had to be well out of reach of her young siblings' grubby hands.

The children were racing around the table with happy shrieks when Leda appeared. She grabbed a younger brother to stop him chasing the oldest boy, plopped him in his seat, and snatched a butter knife away from her smallest sister as she ran past.

"Those aren't toys, Ava."

Her mother brushed past her with a loving smile.

"Thank you Leda. Start slicing the bread, will you? Your father should be here any minute now."

The candles on the table flared to life when her mother walked past, bouncing with a sudden flame. At Mama's command, the rest of children dutifully took their seats, in which they remained, anchored by magic. Bronwyn, the second oldest girl, walked around the table setting out plates.

"Did you get some studying done?" she asked Leda.

"Yes. A little."

A familiar sensation filled Leda's mind, occupying her awareness. An image swam before her; the family was eating dinner, half the stew was gone, and the little boys were laughing. A new picture flashed by right after; Papa walked in the door, dripping rain. Before she could understand it, another one took it's place. Dinner had finished. Bronwyn and Leda were clearing the dishes. Mama was chasing the youngest, trying to get stockings on before bed. A new image came and Papa stepped in, his head down and clothes drenched, a troubled look in his eyes. Of the two pictures, the last left the strongest feeling.

Leda's heart stumbled.

Not bad news. Not today. Not today of all days.

"Papa is going to be late," Leda said as the sensation ebbed away, purposely leaving out the foreboding feeling it gave her. Mama looked up for a moment, surprised. Then the look faded from her green eyes, and she managed an unaffected smile. She wiped her red hands on her apron and nodded, but Leda couldn't hide anything from her. Mama knew something wasn't right.

Leda continued to saw at the bread while Bronwyn ladled out the stew. Papa was supposed to talk to his partners at work today about getting paid in advance so Leda could go away to school. The bad news certainly meant that they wouldn't get the needed sacrans to pay. She shook away the bleak thoughts.

No. This isn't happening. There's no bad news tonight. Only good news.

The Foresight curse that Leda had lived with since infancy activated, raising even more glimpses of future possibilities. Most of the images were of events that could happen soon, some of them were far off possibilities, and none were guaranteed. The curse normally simmered in the background of her mind, but it had a way of coming to the surface when her emotions took over. Although occasionally convenient, it usually felt more like a living nightmare.

Right then, so many possibilities shuffled past her that she had a hard time distinguishing them all. Every event had second- and third-order effects, which occasionally flickered through the mix. Sometimes she saw further than that, to fourth-order effects. In Papa's case, however, she couldn't see the original cause, so the future possibilities became confusing. A building she'd never seen. Sitting at the kitchen table years from now, teaching her siblings. Wiping her mother's face with a rag. Chatham Castle and all the resplendent flower gardens and gazebo.

"Leda?"

Leda shook her head, breaking out of her reverie. When her eyes refocused, Mama was staring at her. Her tired eyes seemed to ask, *Is everything okay?*

"Sorry, Mama. I was lost in my thoughts."

"Leda does that all the time," six-year-old Anthony said. His body bounced up and down as he swung his legs. He balanced a spoon on his nose and spoke with measured words. "She's always spacing out."

Bronwyn set his bowl in front of him, her brown bangs falling into her face.

"Eat."

Leda tried not to focus on her visions when she was around the little kids. They didn't know about her curse, just Bronwyn and her parents. Dinner was relatively quiet, despite the usual bickering and banter. As usual, Bronwyn remained silent, speaking only when Mama addressed her. Leda said nothing.

Every minute that passed narrowed the possibilities. Leda saw herself at Mama and Papa's bedroom door with Bronwyn, listening through the thick wood. Talking to Mama and Papa in front of the fire came next. Neither of them felt stronger. At this point, Papa must be deciding whether he should talk to Mama first, or include Leda and Bronwyn in the conversation right away. He hadn't decided. Leda hoped for the second.

Once all the kids were done they shot off towards their rooms as if blighters—magic balls of energy—followed at their heels, chasing them into their pajamas. Mama stood up, and putting a hand under their chins, kissed both Leda and Bronwyn's cheeks.

"Thank you, my girls. I don't know what I'd do without you."

Bronwyn's deep brown eyes glowed.

"We'll clean up, Mama," she offered. "Go rest. You've been up all day."

Mama smiled one last time and placed a hand on the small of her back. Her swollen tummy was beginning to stick out in earnest now. It wouldn't be much longer before Mama would have to cut back on work, putting the chores onto Bronwyn and Leda. A sense of dread stirred in Leda's gut.

Taking care of her family would seriously cut into her time to study for the interview, which was coming soon. The interview was the only way to get into Miss Mabel's School for Girls, which could be Leda's ticket out of the tired village of Hansham, and Leda wanted it bad. She'd show them. She'd be so intelligent that the Watcher Isadora couldn't stand to turn her away.

Of course, that would only work if her family could prove they had the money to send her away for three years, which was probably the biggest challenge of all. Papa planned to ask for an advance on his pay, but due to the depressing future possibilities Leda had just seen, she began to have doubts. Would she be able to go to Miss Mabel's?

Everything in her future depended on this interview. If Leda didn't go to Miss Mabel's School for Girls, she'd be forced into a life like her mother's. Poor. Scraping by on the dregs of leftovers just to feed her family.

That wouldn't happen.

Bronwyn gathered the leftover bread crusts like the steady girl that she was and peered into the cauldron that was once bubbling with stew. Papa would crumble the crusts into his soup, so she set them aside on his plate and turned her large eyes on Leda as they collected the dirty dinner plates.

"Is everything okay with Papa, Leedee?" she asked in a quiet voice. Leda scowled at the sound of her childhood nickname but could hear real anxiety in Bronwyn's query, so she didn't chastise her.

"Yes. I think something happened at work."

Bronwyn paled in seconds. Her voice was raspy when she spoke. "Did Papa lose his job?"

"No." Leda's forehead gathered in frustration. "At least, I don't think so. I can't tell. I can't see the past."

Bronwyn took in a deep breath, resolving herself for whatever came, but the pinched look remained in her face.

"Let's hope not."

Leda glanced around. *Yes,* she thought. *Let's hope not. We can't afford to get any poorer than we are now.* Affirming her thought, a gust of wind blew against the house, sending a light whistle through the loose window panes. Leda looked at the limp, stained drapes, the uneven table, and the old wooden bucket they washed the dishes in. A dilapidated mess, all of it.

Sensing her thoughts, Bronwyn shot her a narrow look. Of all the children, she was the most sensitive over the family poverty.

"I know what you're thinking," she said.

"Oh really?"

"You're thinking about how poor we are, and you're worried that whatever happened has something to do with you going to Miss Mabel's."

Hearing Bronwyn say it like that made Leda's insides tighten with shame, but she didn't deny it because it was true. The sight of Papa walking up the back path flashed through her eyes, followed by a wave of certainty that told her he had returned.

"Papa's here."

A few seconds later the door swung open. Papa looked up, his blonde hair pasted to his face, fatigued eyes drawn into low angles. His smile took great effort and didn't reach his eyes.

"Hello, girls."

Bronwyn immediately rushed to help him out of his wet coat. Leda placed the stack of dried plates in the cupboard, watching Papa closely from the corner of her eyes.

"Are you all right Papa? You're late," Bronwyn said.

"Yes, just held back for a little meeting is all."

A little meeting that decides my future, Leda wanted to add.

Mama and three of the children emerged from the bedrooms. The kids squealed with excitement, throwing themselves into Papa's wet body and climbing up his leg.

"Oh, Reginald, you're soaking wet," Mama said. "You'd better change before you get sick."

He ruffled heads and kissed a few cheeks, dutifully listening to the reports of all the childish adventures of the day. Then Mama herded the children into their respective beds after they told Papa good night. Within minutes the kitchen was empty again. Bronwyn sighed and returned to the dirty dishes, that relentless master which never seemed to end.

Papa came back just as Leda and Bronwyn finished drying the last dish. Bronwyn grabbed the bowl of stew from its place by the fire and set it in front of him.

"Oh, what a long day! This smells like a fine stew, Bronwyn. Thank you."

She smiled in adoration and sat down across from him. Mama settled into the rocking chair nearby, leaned her head back, and closed her eyes with her hands on her round belly.

"Why were you late, Papa?" Leda asked. She stood across from him, gripping a chair in her hands, seeking balance.

Don't say they won't pay you early. Don't say they won't pay you early.

He didn't look at her but paused in thought, staring at his bowl with a frown.

"I had a few things to clear up."

"Is everything all right?" Mama asked, opening her eyes when Papa hesitated. He paused, thinking, and then turned to Leda.

"No. It's not."

Leda's heart plummeted into her stomach. *This can't be happening. Attending Miss Mabel's has been my only dream, my only request.*

Don't take this away from me.

Papa took a drink of water and then continued. "I spoke with the other witches at work today about getting the sacrans in advance to pay for Miss Mabel's, but they said no. Even if they had, the cost is more than we have saved, what with the new baby coming."

His gaze softened and he looked right at her. "We can't afford to send you, Leda. Not this year, anyway."

Her heart started to crinkle, pulling from the inside out. Her chest felt like a wall of rock, unable to expand so she could breathe.

We can't afford to send you.

The curse took over, sending her mind into a nonsensical blur of overwhelming images and possibilities. She let it take her away. An escape. An alternate kind of reality. The thick plug of tears in her throat and the sound of her desperate gasp brought Leda out of it. Bronwyn stared at her lap, playing with the edge of her apron, unable to meet her eyes.

"I'm so sorry, Leda," Papa continued. "I know how much this means to you."

No, you don't. You could never know.

She stepped away from the table with a shaky breath, her eyes averted.

"Leda, please stop."

But she didn't. She turned, walked calmly to her bedroom, and closed the door behind her. Outside, rain dropped down the window-pane in liquid shadows. She drew a deep breath and lowered herself onto the makeshift bed. The whirling future abated a little.

"No tears," she chanted. "No tears."

Her mother's voice filtered through the door.

"Just leave her, Reginald. Give her a few moments."

"I want to—"

"An explanation won't help. Not right now. Trust me. Let her be."

Yes, Leda thought. *An explanation will only take away all hope. At least this way I can pretend. I can still imagine that I'll attend Miss Mabel's, that I'll be someone, that I won't be stuck in the cycle of my family, drowning because no one knows who I am.*

Even as she thought it, she knew it was a lie. With eight mouths to feed, and another on the way, the sacrans were already stretched further than they could go. Her heart filled her throat as a lone tear fell off her cheek and landed on the back of her hand.

Leda woke to a pale pink sky and a numb left arm. She stared out the window, and with a bitter sigh wished it would be ugly weather instead.

The soft sounds of Mama moving about reminded her that the day had to begin. The sight of Mama in the kitchen flapped through Leda's head, bringing with it hundreds of other possibilities. All of the visuals were of the same familiar routine. Bread. Sweeping. Chasing a sibling. Hunkering down in the cupboard. Walking to the village to run an errand for Mama.

Leda had cried herself to sleep in her work dress, so she crept out of bed and made her way straight to the kitchen without a sound. The fire in the grate snapped and popped, heating a cauldron of break-fast mash. Leda walked away from the unappealing gray mass, her hunger stricken. What she wouldn't have given for a fresh handful of strawberries!

"Hey Leedee," Mama said, taking a blob of dough from where it had been rising near the fire and carried it to the table. Flour speckled her apron and arms.

"Do you need help?"

"No."

Startled, Leda looked up in question. Mama motioned towards the chair beside her workspace. Her hands kneaded into the ball of dough, occasionally slapping a bit of flour onto it, leaving dustings on her arms and cheeks.

"You help with every meal, Leda. You deserve a break. Why don't you sit and talk to me?"

"I don't want to talk about—"

"I know. But we're going to talk about it anyway."

Leda sat down and stared at the floor, but Mama grabbed her chin with a gentle touch and turned her face upwards. Leda could feel the soft grit of the flour on her jawline.

"I'm sorry about the news you had last night."

"I know."

"I also know that you're scared that not attending Miss Mabel's will mean you'll end up like me."

Leda's eyes widened with both shock and fear. A rush of future images came from her sudden emotions. Mama crying. The baby born. Bronwyn wearing an unfamiliar uniform. Leda took in a deep breath and forced herself to calm. The visions retreated, granting her room to think.

"Don't try to tell me it isn't true," Mama said before Leda could get a word in. "I can see it in your eyes. You think I'm trapped in this life. You think I'm strapped to raising children and living a life of poverty, and you don't want that for yourself. Am I right?"

The pictures started whistling past again. Foraging through the forest. Talking to Bronwyn. Leda raked a hand through her hair in frustration. The curse was so much stronger than her! It took several long minutes to get her mind back. Mama waited, understanding, like no one else ever did.

"Yes Mama," she finally whispered.

"Just because I got married at a very young age and started my family right away doesn't mean that you have to take the same path. You have very different strengths and talents than me."

Leda was afraid to look at her, worried Mama'd take it all back and verify her biggest fear.

"Really?" she finally managed to ask.

Mama laughed. It was a low, quiet sound that wrapped Leda's heart in comfort. She crouched down and put a floury arm around Leda's shoulder. A part of Leda's heart repaired itself.

"Of course not, Leda! You're destined for far greater things than I wanted to do. You have too much talent, and too much drive, to stay in this little village."

Leda's momentary joy and spark of hope began to deflate.

"But that's impossible now."

"Is it?"

Mama's voice rose with her question. For a split second Leda doubted her own resolve; was her dream impossible?

"You could earn the money," Mama suggested.

Leda scoffed. "Right. It's spring. School starts in the fall."

Mama remained uncowed by her skeptical display and simply pressed her lips together. She straightened up, brushing the flour off Leda's worn dress.

"I know there's a few ideas that have been percolating in your head for a while now. A couple of challenging potions?"

With a gasp, Leda's mind flashed to the the Forgotten Potion. Would it be possible?

"But I don't have the ingredients," she said slowly, "or a place to make it. We could never do it here. Not with all the kids."

"Make it happen."

Mama returned to the bread, humming under her breath, and left Leda to her thoughts, which churned in wild abandon.

Make it happen.

Her mind slipped into the ready images flashing through it, sending her down twenty different paths. A library at an unfamiliar school, a uniform she didn't recognize. Standing in the kitchen, children surrounding her. Working at the grocers' in Hansham. None of them were connected completely, and all of them were hazy.

But the fact that she saw them meant there was a chance.

She shot off the chair, kissed her mother on the cheek, grabbed her threadbare cloak, and ran for the village.

Three days later, Leda stared at her bubbling brew with an up-turned lip.

"Hey Leda!" her best friend Camille called, hopping up into the shack with a jaunty hop. She instantly reared back.

"Whoa! What ith that thmell?" Camille asked, plugging her nose with one hand while fanning the air with the other. "Ith that yer pothun?"

"Yes," Leda said with a frustrated sigh. "It's the Forgotten Potion."

"The one you're going to thell to earn money for thcool? Are you thure anyone will buy it? It thmells like rotten cheese."

"Yes."

"Could you get a bigger cauldron? Jikes, Leda, that's mathive," Camille said, peering in over the top and grimacing again.

"It's the only one I could find," Leda mumbled, embarrassed. In truth, the cauldron was quite large for such a small brew. The potion simmered on the bottom, barely visible, lost to the grand blackness. "Anyway, the size of the cauldron doesn't matter. The only thing I'm worried about is finishing before Isadora comes for the interview. If I don't have the potion, I have no proof that we can afford it."

Camille rolled her eyes.

"You'll be accthepted, Leda," she said, taking another step back, eyes watering. "Whew. That really thtinks!"

"For now." Right then, Leda was willing to endure just about any-thing. "It'll smell like juniper once it's done."

Camille gazed around the small shed Leda had talked the grocer into letting her borrow. The trees and vines of Letum Wood had all but consumed the forgotten shack, making it a perfect spot to leave a potion to brew, unseen by prying eyes.

"Nice place," Camille muttered with another step back, eyeing the questionable integrity of the rotting boards and unplugging her nose in the safer air outside. "Sure it's not going to fall in on you?"

Leda ignored the question, although she'd had that same thought herself. But the visions in Leda's head didn't show a collapsed shack, so she felt confident it would hold up. All the images she saw had narrowed considerably in the past three days of potion work, and so far the brew was right on track.

"Anyway," Camille sang, "I just wanted to stop by and see if you got the letter from Isadora."

Leda froze.

"What letter?"

"Telling us that she had to change the date. She'll be here tomorrow." Camille's expression dropped into sudden concern. "Oh, wait. Is the potion going to be ready by then?"

Leda whirled around.

"What?" she screeched. "Isadora will be here tomorrow?"

Startled, Camille's hazel eyes widened.

"Y-yes," she said, pulling a small envelope from her pocket. "Here's the letter."

Leda nearly tore it in half trying to take the bit of parchment from the envelope. To her horror, it confirmed Camille's announcement.

I will arrive tomorrow morning for the interviews. Please have Leda and Camille meet me at the apothecary.

"Camille!" Leda cried in dismay. "This is terrible! The potion needs at least two more days."

"Can't you speed it up at all?"

"No!" Her hands raked through her hair. "This is awful!"

Camille chewed her bottom lip. "What if we go ask Fitz? He'll know what to do!"

Fitz was the eccentric, twiggy potionmaker that holed up in the apothecary. Leda stopped and stared at Camille. Fitz was an option. Not a good one, but an option.

"Would he help?" Leda asked.

Camille shrugged. "Maybe. Worth a try, right?"

Fitz wouldn't be happy to see her, but Leda didn't care.

"Yes," she said, recovering her breath. The curse whirled through her mind. She had to stop and close her eyes against the relentless shuffle of images. Elderberries. An old woman. A cottage. Elderberries again.

Leda shook her head to clear her thoughts. *No, no, no,* she told herself. *Not elderberry! Too dangerous.*

"Let's go," she said with a grim tone. Camille squared her shoulders like a Guardian preparing for battle.

"Right. I'll lead the way."

"What do you want?" Fitz asked as Leda stepped into his office at the apothecary. A pair of glasses covered his large blue eyes, but only one of them held a lens, which magnified his pupil so that it filled the entire circle. When he blinked it looked like his eye disappeared and then reappeared again.

"I need some help," Leda responded.

Fitz lifted a thin eyebrow. He was built tall and skinny, much like a glass vial, and with about as much personality.

"I don't like helping people," he said.

"I know."

Fitz was known all around the village for his peculiar eyeglasses and bad moods. The only things anyone had ever seen him eat were raw apples and cups of coffee. As a result, he often seemed moody and jittery, but no one was ever sure if it was because he'd had too much that day, or not enough.

"Then why did you come?" he asked.

"Advice."

He rolled his eyes and turned away but kept Leda within his line of sight. Taking it as permission, she continued.

"I'm making the Forgotten Potion."

She knew he'd be skeptical, but his blank reaction wasn't what she'd expected. He just stared at her, his great eye blinking up and down.

"And I have to finish it by tomorrow," she concluded when he

13

didn't react. "The potion needs two more days. Can I increase the heat to cut down the brewing time?"

"No. You aren't going to finish it," he said. "You can't shortcut a potion. Increasing the temperature will change the viscosity and ruin the brew."

"There's got to be a way around it!"

"There is. Pick a different potion."

"It's too late for that."

"I can't help you." He turned and started walking towards the door. Leda hurled herself in front of him, blocking his path. In her desperation she was willing to submit one more option, a plan that surely testified to her distress.

"What if I add elderberry?" she asked.

He stopped.

"What?"

"Elderberry. What if I add it? It will speed up the process. I could increase the heat as well, making it finish by morning."

His forehead furrowed in thought. "You want to add elderberry to a weak potion in order to speed up the brewing time?"

"Yes."

"It won't work," he concluded, after a long silence. "Your potion would be too volatile to trust. It would explode."

"What if I—"

"No." He shot her a warning glare. "Forget it, Leda. You can't do the Forgotten Potion."

"But everything depends on this! I'm going to sell it to pay tuition to Miss Mabel's School for Girls. If I don't get this, I'll be a nobody!"

He paused, staring into her desperate face with all the warmth of an arctic breeze.

"There's nothing I can do to help you."

Frustrated, Leda spun on her heel, stalked past Camille, strode through the forest, and out to the little shed. The potion bubbled on, releasing a citrusy scent. It was right on track and looking perfect. If only it could finish sooner!

She scrounged through her herb chest and retrieved the packet of elderberry from the bottom.

Dare I?

She had enough to do the job and then some. Leda hesitated, sifting out a sprinkling of the herb into her palm. The stakes were the highest they had ever been. But elderberry? Was she that desperate to escape her life? She gazed down at her tattered dress and holey shoes.

Yes. Yes, I am that despereate.

With an decisive breath, Leda dropped the elderberry into the pot. The top of the brew fizzled into a thousand bubbles, then settled, returning to the usual boil.

Leda took a step back.

Elderberry was a fickle herb to work with. From this point on, stirring the potion or touching the pot would only alter the reaction. Her heart slammed in her chest. It had a few hours to work overnight. Isadora would arrive in the morning for the interview. The potion had to be ready. The massive cauldron seemed to mock her.

This won't work. Fitz is right.

No. Fitz was wrong. He must be wrong. Elderberry would speed up the process. It wouldn't explode.

If it did, it would take her future with it.

Leda woke to the sound of giggling.

She shot out of bed, disoriented by the rays of light streaming through her window. Leda always woke up before the sun to start breakfast with Bronwyn. The sun meant morning, which meant that the interview with Isadora was upon her.

"Oh no," she cried, shoving her hair out of her face. "I slept in. I slept in!"

Bronwyn stirred next to her beneath a layer of blankets. She let out a moan as Leda threw the covers off and vaulted out of bed.

"Bronwyn! Wake up! I slept in! Isadora is going to be in town any minute now!"

Leda stumbled into the dining room with her shoes in hand, pulling a dress over her head at the same time. Mama was wrangling the little children into their seats.

"Leda, what are you doing here?" Mama asked, looking up. "I thought you left hours ago."

"Obviously not!" Leda yelled. "Why didn't you wake me?"

She pushed past the kids, snatching her shoulder bag from the hook in the wall. Her youngest brother gave a wail when she ignored his outstretched arms and drooling lower lip.

"What can I do?" Mama cried after her, but Leda was already gone, the door slamming behind her.

Leda's heart fell into her stomach with a heavy lurch as she approached the sleepy town of Hansham. A few buildings were awake, small plumes of smoke spiraling up from the brick chimneys. Letum Wood's expansive canopy soaked up much of the light, filtering the rest through the many leaves to fall in solitary beams. The sight of a small crowd of witches at the apothecary sent a whirl of pictures through her mind.

"No," she muttered, bracing her head with one hand. "Not now! Infernal curse."

The queue of witches murmured and jostled each other. Having two girls this close to getting into a Network school meant the whole town had to stick their nose in it. Leda muttered at them under her breath. She hated gossip.

"Hey," she growled, shouldering her way to the front. "Let me through!"

An old woman with a curved back and low shoulders stood next to Mr Hymas, the apothecary. Camille rushed to Leda's side, her dishwater blonde curls bouncing on her neck.

"Where have you been?" she cried. "We've been waiting for almost ten minutes."

"I accidentally slept in. What's happening? Am I too late? What about the interview?"

"Isadora is just discussing a few things with Mr. Hymas." Camille looked over her shoulder to the little shed behind the apothecary and then back to Leda. "Is your potion ready?" she whispered.

Leda's mouth was so dry from fear that she worried sand would spill from the corners. There was no telling. Her plan had been to wake up early and check on it, but now she'd have to trust fate.

"I hope so," she said with a trembling voice.

Isadora's eyes found Leda, sending a cold wash of fear down her skin.

"Merry meet, Leda," she called.

"Merry meet, Miss Isadora," Leda said, ducking her head before looking back up. Were Isadora's eyes different colors? Leda blinked several times. No, surely they couldn't be. Leda had never met another person with eyes like her own.

"Are you ready?" Isadora asked.

What little composure Leda had left failed. Her curse accelerated the spinning images, and she could barely get enough control to think. She managed a terse nod.

"I understand you've made a very difficult potion," Isadora said as Leda joined her. "Would you mind if I looked at it?"

"No, I wouldn't mind."

"I'll follow you."

Isadora motioned for her to start. Mr. Hymas managed to control the crowd, keeping them at the apothecary with an offer of free spiced tea. His voice rang out through the trees, following Leda and Isadora until it faded behind them.

Despite her gnarly joints and hunched appearance, Isadora moved with surprising speed. Leda didn't speak. Her nerves and emotions were too strong to allow any forethought. Instead, all she saw were blurry, indistinguishable flashes of light and darkness. Her head began to pound. When they arrived, Leda hesitated outside of the hut.

"Is there a problem?" Isadora asked.

Yes. No. I don't know.

"No." Leda heard her voice respond before her brain was aware. "This is where I prepared my potion."

"What potion did you make?"

"The Forgotten Potion."

This time Leda looked to judge Isadora's reaction. The deep lines of her old face shifted.

"Oh? What for?"

"I had planned to sell it for tuition money so that when you came I'd be able to prove that I could go." Leda could barely choke the words out.

Isadora hummed something under her breath. "I see. What made you decide to do the Forgotten Potion? It's very difficult."

"I needed something valuable."

"There are many valuable potions that aren't quite so challenging."

Leda tried to push the embarrassment down, but it moved into her voice instead, making her sound raspy.

"I needed a rare, valuable potion. My family doesn't have the money to send me to Miss Mabel's, and I knew this would get me enough."

Isadora studied her expression.

"Your eyes are two different colors," Isadora observed. Taken aback by the sudden shift in conversation, Leda simply blinked.

"I—"

Then Isadora smiled.

"So are mine."

Leda looked closer. So she hadn't imagined it. Isadora had one eye that was a shade of gold, like a deep amber, while the other was jade green.

"Yes," Leda whispered, "you do."

"It's a rare trait, you know."

"Does it mean something?"

"It can."

"Would you like to see my potion?" Leda asked, feeling sick. She just wanted this over with.

"Yes, I'm quite intrigued."

Leda drew in a deep breath, gave the handle a pull, and let the door swing open. She stifled a gasp of shock.

A melted lump of black had replaced the massive cauldron. The sides curled down like the petals of a dying flower. A rough, jagged layer of sparkling crystals coated every surface, from the floor to the ceiling, in a dark shimmer. Only a few boards were visible in between the coats of black. Isadora's eyebrows lifted.

"Oh," she whispered, putting a hand on the doorframe. "Oh my."

They gaped at the disaster together. Leda wasn't sure if she wanted to laugh or cry. Her future had exploded in a mess of shining black shards. Literally exploded. She wasn't even sure if it would come off the walls, or the jars, or the broom in the corner. Fitz had been right after all.

Domestic tranquility, here I come.

Leda opened her mouth to explain but realized she didn't know what to say and closed it again.

"Goodness. It's been a while since I've seen such a big collection of Leigh crystal," Isadora said, running her fingertips along the jagged edges nearest her. "Actually, I'm not sure I've ever seen this much."

Leda's breath caught. Leigh crystal?

"What?"

Isadora shot Leda a look from the corner of her eye.

"Yes. For how valuable it is, very few know the potion. Even fewer are brave enough to attempt making it due to the explosive nature of the process, as you can see. Your big cauldron must have contained the reaction."

Leigh crystal.

The realization slapped her in the face. Leigh crystal was a magical imitation of black crystal, but it looked so real, and was so much easier to manipulate, that most witches used it instead. Even as an imitation, it was a difficult potion to execute well.

"Leigh crystal. Yes," Leda murmured. Oh, she wished she hadn't told Isadora that she was trying the Forgotten Potion! Then she could have pretended like Leigh crystal had been the objective and Isadora would see how clever she could be.

"Well, this was certainly a surprise." Isadora drew in a deep breath, and looked over at Leda. "One that I would say demonstrates a fair amount of talent . . . and a fair amount of heart."

"What?" Leda asked, turning to her in shock.

"I'm quite impressed."

"But why?" Leda asked. "I got it all wrong!"

"Success at Miss Mabel's is about more than just potions. It's about working hard for what you want."

"But I didn't even get the potion that I wanted."

"Maybe not, but you tried. I don't need to see or hear anymore. You are very bright, I can see that. Motivated as well, if not isolating and prone to anger. Those can all be worked with. Welcome to Miss Mabel's School for Girls, Leda. I'd love to purchase all of this Leigh from you, but I can't afford it. I know a witch who would be interested in buying all of it, but we can discuss that later."

Leda just stared at her, frozen and shocked.

"You're going to let me in?"

"If you will agree." Isadora cast her eyes around the small hut. "I think you have enough Leigh to pay your way through and possibly a little more."

Leda hesitated, her mouth open. This had been an accident. Luck wouldn't help her pass. The Leigh crystal didn't prove she was talented, or even had heart. All this showed was that she was desperate to escape her life.

"Miss Isadora, I—"

"Will be wonderful, I'm sure."

"Thank you, but—"

"I've been doing this for over fifty years now, Leda." There was a gentle tone of chiding in Isadora's tone. "In that time, I've met thousands of girls, tens of thousands, probably. All of those I've chosen have succeeded in the school. I've never made a mistake."

"This was an accident," Leda admitted, gesturing to the hut.

"Perhaps. But your determination and intellect are not."

"Never?" Leda asked after a small stretch of silence. "You've never made a mistake?"

Isadora gave her a toothy smile.

"Never."

Camille

Bettina cleared her throat as she took a sip of black currant tea. She did it before every single sip. Just as she read the mail every morning over the same type of tea, in the same cup. Routine was life, and Aunt Bettina lived it well. She wore the same black dress, the same stern bun, and the same apathetic air. She was small boned, with a thin frame, graying blonde hair, and sharp eyes. Bettina's unwavering lack of change was enough to make fifteen-year-old Camille dotty.

Worse still was Aunt Angie, who sat at the far end of the table, her right index finger constantly lifted to her upper lip with a handkerchief wrapped around it. Her nose ran all year, rain or shine, forcing her to sniffle every two-and-a-half minutes. Camille didn't doubt that her two aunts were good people, but she imagined they were better in smaller doses.

"Once I finish the mail," Bettina said, without looking up from the current letter, "we will start your first algebra lesson."

"Algebra?" Camille groaned, earning a sharp look of reprimand. She forced away a frown and lightened her tone. "Is there something else we can try?"

"Absolutely not."

Camille tightened her jaw and steeled herself for another long day.

With a methodical air, Bettina lifted a scroll with her left hand, took it in her right, undid the twine tie with her left, took another sip of tea, had a careful bite of biscuit, took another measured sip, set the cup down, then tugged on the parchment, and peered at the words over the top of her half-moon glasses.

Camille watched the ritual with detached interest.

I'm going to fall asleep at the breakfast table, and then she'll make me sit in the chair again, staring at the wall.

"Can I work on my sewing instead?"

"You do need some work with your stitches," Angie whispered, eyes flickering over her plate half-full of breakfast. She gazed off, out the window, wandering vapidly into lands that no one else could see. Camille wished she'd drink more of her *special tonic* and slip further into the stupor that usually claimed her.

Knowing she could do nothing but wait for the algebraic torture to begin, Camille settled back in her chair with a sigh. Once Bettina finished the letter, she folded it up and looked to her niece. Camille gave her a hopeful, pleading look.

"Yes," Bettina said, "you may work on your sewing."

Camille perked up.

"After you start algebra," Bettina clarified, robbing Camille's hope and leaving her more depressed than ever.

"Oh Bettina, please, no!"

"Your math skills need work, Camille."

Bettina started the ritual over with another letter. Realizing she'd lost the battle once again, Camille sighed, propped her chin on her hand, and gazed out the window. There never was conversation over tea. Or at any time, for that matter. She wished she could at least go outside, where white blossoms had sprouted on the trees. They were so lovely and frail, like delicate porcelin cups balancing on twigs. Unlike the drab house, with little color and no warmth. Camille longed to sit in the sun.

"Well," said Bettina, with a low hum of surprise in her voice. She pulled the letter away from her face and peered at it over the top of her glasses, as if that would help her see it. "I wasn't expecting this."

Both Camille and Angie looked up. It had been a long time since Bettina had been surprised about anything. Camille was too shocked to move, worried it might break the moment.

Bettina readjusted her position on the chair, but said no more.

Her forehead scrunched into heavy lines, making her thin face appear asymmetrical. Angie looked away, her attention already elsewhere. Camille waited, fists clenched. It had something to do with her—she could feel it.

"What is it, Aunt Bettina?" she asked in a prim tone.

"The letter is from the Network."

"What?" Camille asked.

Angie perked up, showing more life than she had all morning.

"Is my new tincture of blessed thistle in? I haven't been able to eat well since my last supply ran out. This indigestion is horrible."

"No, it's not about your tincture. The letter is in regards to Camille."

I knew it! Camille thought, her heart fluttering. *I knew it was about me!*

Bettina looked over her glasses again, staring straight into Camille's eyes.

"Isadora is coming to town. This confirms your interview."

"Interview?" She repeated the word as if it were foreign. "Isadora?"

Had they delivered the letter here on accident? Leda was the only one interviewing with Isadora. She'd been talking about it for months.

"I signed you up for an interview that will determine if you can attend Miss Mabel's School for Girls. I didn't tell you because I didn't want to hear you talking about it all the time. Isadora will be here five days hence."

Camille felt faint. The room swam before her eyes and she grabbed the edge of the table. Attend Miss Mabel's School for Girls? Wasn't that the dream of every girl in the village, in all of Antebellum? On the verge of hyperventilating, she took several slow, deep breaths.

"Oh, Aunt Bettina, I'd love to go!" Camille found her tongue in a mad rush of words. "I'll do whatever I have too! I'll do my algebra. I'll improve my sewing. I'll work longer hours at the bakery—"

Her spinning dreams slowed to a standstill when she took in Bettina's stiff shoulders and pursed lips. Angie's tea cup trembled as she lifted it to drink, then abandoned her goal halfway through and set it down to return to her vague dreams.

"Camille, there's something you need to think about before you do this. Are you listening?" Bettina asked.

"Of course."

"Miss Mabel's is an advanced school for witches that involves serious studying. The good gods know I've debated whether I should have done this, whether you're up to the challenge, but I can't take it back now. It's no secret that you don't love studying and have the attention span of a four-year-old."

The familiar feeling of loneliness and hurt crept over Camille. Bettina wanted to get rid of her, to send her away to school and restore the perfect balance of the silent house. It was all she could do to keep her tears under control.

"You don't think I would study?" Camille asked, unable to keep the wounded look from her eyes.

"I didn't say that, Camille. I simply said you'll need to work harder than you do now."

I'd do anything to get away from here! I can't study when it's so quiet.

"I will," she promised, and she meant it more than anything. There was nothing she wanted more than to leave and never see Bettina's infernal rituals ever again.

"Then we need to discuss what you plan to study," Bettina said, setting the scroll aside. "You must have a purpose, a plan. Otherwise it'll just be your usual chaotic madness, and you'll have no motivation."

Camille wanted to say it wasn't true but bit the inside of her cheek instead.

"I don't know yet," she finally said.

Bettina shot her a sharp look and took the last careful sip of tea.

"Figure it out before you go. No one likes a student without focus."

Or a world without color, like this one.

"Yes Bettina," she mumbled. "May I go?"

"Yes," Bettina said in a low tone, "you may go."

Camille burst from the chair with a gusto that made it clatter and nearly fall. She ignored the warning glare from Bettina and left the house, and all of its anxiety, behind her.

"She wants to get rid of me."

Camille popped a flower off a nearby stem, and pressed it to her nose. The petals felt like the gentle caress of a fingertip. She closed her eyes and imagined her mother there, listening to her, advising her.

"She wants to be rid of me so badly that she's trying to send me to a school she doesn't think I qualify for."

No, her mother would say with a warm smile, tucking a stray lock of hair behind her ear. *That's not it at all. Bettina and Angie love you, they just don't know how to show it. And I love you too. You'll be wonderful at Miss Mabel's, Cammie. You'll be the loveliest girl there, with all the same pretty dresses and scarves to match them.*

"You're probably right," Leda's pragmatic tone swooped in instead, shattering Camille's vision of her mother and bringing her crashing back to reality. "You do tend to make Bettina crazy. But at least she's sending you."

Her unspoken words hung between them.

And you can afford to go.

Camille's hand fell to her side, away from her face. The disappointment was acute. Leda was far too logical to understand the haunting emptiness of Bettina's house.

"Yes," Camille sighed, knowing Leda would never see it her way. "I suppose you're right."

They sat on an old swing tethered to a gazebo in the middle of Hansham. It could hardly be called a town—little more than a village, if that. A vague dirt road ambled down the middle, creating a kind of main street. The apothecary stood at the end, where Mr. Hymas, the Coven leader for this part of Letum Wood, worked. He lived above it with his wife, and was a well-groomed, charismatic witch that should have lived in a city but loved the woods far too much.

The grocer's stall stood next to the apothecary, looking shabby in comparison. Miss Kathy's bakery brought up the end of the road, the chimney puffing away with a thin stream of smoke. Camille sniffed.

Vanilla almond cookies today, she thought, her stomach grumbling.

She wished it were chocolate, or caramel. Those always made her feel better.

In the distance, a blacksmith pounded away on some horseshoes. It was a cozy scene to any newcomer, but a dull prison to both girls, who saw it every day. Their houses, like those of most witches in the area, were well-hidden in Letum Wood, ensconced in the verdant trees, accessible by footpath or a small road wide enough only to admit a horse and buggy.

After a few seconds of silence that Camille was certain had really been several minutes, she blurted out the question that lay heavily on her mind.

"Please, Leda?" she pleaded. "Please look ahead for me?"

Leda let out a long sigh.

"Camille, you know—"

"I know how you feel about looking into the future!" she quickly said, turning to Leda and grabbing her arm. "I know! But I'm so nervous, Leda. This is my chance to get away from Bettina, and Angie, and their horrid silent house with no color or anything pretty. Please?"

For an eternity, Leda searched her friend's eyes, looking as if she'd waver on her rigid rule. Then she pulled her arm away from Camille's tight grasp.

"No," she finally said, looking away, jaw set. Camille slumped back against the swing, tilted her head up and stared into the verdant canopy above. Leda had been more distracted than usual lately, what with the interview on her mind. Camille knew she wasn't in the mood to talk, but then, Leda never was.

"I'm afraid," Camille admitted, envisioning a future full of gray walls and Bettina's rituals. "Even though it's still a few days away now."

"I know," Leda said, swallowing, and Camille wondered if Leda was trying to stop herself from admitting that she was frightened too.

The day of Isadora's interview came all too soon.

One minute Camille was staring at a ceiling lit by early morning light, her stomach churning so much she was going to be sick, and then Mr. Hymas was leading her into his office where Isadora waited, whispering a quick, "Good luck," as she walked inside.

Camille stood in front of the chair, refusing to sit down. At least, she didn't want to. But the chair seemed to reach up and grab her, forcing her to sit with a heavy thump while Isadora looked on.

Only answer the questions, Camille coached herself. *Don't prattle on like you normally do. She'll ask questions, you answer. Just like meals with Bettina and Angie, although Angie never asks you questions. She takes far too much of that medication to ask lucid questions—*

"Merry meet, Camille," Isadora said, interrupting her internal dialogue.

Camille startled, managing a forced smile.

"Merry meet, Miss Isadora."

Her knees knocked together, causing her white socks to slide down towards her ankles like the wrinkles on a fat worm.

"This is a nice apothecary," Isadora said, gazing around with her aged eyes. Her skin had more lumps than a raisin, and Camille wondered if that was what she'd look like when she got old. She'd prefer not to. Leda's mother was lovely despite having had all of her kids.

"Yes," Camille said for lack of anything else, and gazed around the walls of the back office. An old painting, faded around the edges, filled up one wall. The flowers on it were vibrant and bright despite the wearing effect of time. Vials and jars cluttered the shelves, nearly crowded out by old books tearing at the seams. A stack of parchments climbed the wall.

"Tell me about your aunts," Isadora said.

"Bettina and Angie?" Camille asked in surprise. What could be interesting about them? They hardly ever left the house. "Well, uh, they took me in when my parents died."

"The Kimeral plague," Isadora supplied.

Just hearing the words made Camille visibly shudder.

"Yes," she said, looking down. "I was just a little girl."

"How did you survive?"

"I don't know. One day my parents became sick, and two days later they were gone. Bettina came and brought me back. Hansham is so isolated that it wasn't hit by the plague, luckily. I could have gotten it, but I didn't."

Camille snapped her jaw shut, silently berating herself.

Stop jabbering!

Her eyes fell to the desk, where a small feather raced across an open scroll. A shot of horror made her feel suddenly weak.

She's taking notes!

"What kind of schooling have you had?" Isadora had to ask the question twice before Camille fumbled through a reply.

"H-homeschooling, mostly," she managed after a hefty swallow. "There are no schools this far east. We're too deep in Letum Wood. Mostly my Aunt Bettina taught me. Angie is always too sick, what with her indigestion and all."

Camille, distracted by the feather that never stopped moving, heard herself rambling again but couldn't stop it.

"Have you learned anything about herbs?" Isadora asked, peering into Camille's globe-like hazel eyes.

"Is there a reason you're taking notes?"

The question burst out of Camille's mouth before she could stop it. She wrung her hands together in her lap, knuckles white.

"Am I doing something wrong?"

Isadora just smiled.

"Who said those notes are about you?"

Camille just stared at her, worrying her bottom lip with her teeth.

"Well, I—I just assumed . . . you asked . . . what was the original question?" she asked in a squeak. She couldn't even think straight. That blasted feather never stopped.

"Herbs," Isadora reminded her. "I wondered if you had ever worked with herbs."

"A little bit. I know some herbs because of Leda and Miss Kathy."

Isadora looked up from the diary, her thin eyebrows lifting.

"Have you ever thought of being an apothecary? They work with herbs every now and then."

"Well," Camille hedged. "I thought about it but I just . . . I just . . . it could be a pretty quiet job, don't you think?"

"Could be," Isadora reasoned. "How about a potionmaker, like your friend Fitz?"

"Fitz isn't my friend," Camille gently corrected Isadora. "Besides, potionmakers don't work with people. That's a job for witches like Leda, who are grumpy around other witches and want to work on their own."

Isadora's lip turned up at little at the corner, but she hid it by coughing into her fist.

"And you don't want to work alone."

"No!"

The answer came out far louder and more vehemently than she meant it to. Camille didn't realize that she'd shot forward in her seat until it was too late and sat back with a sheepish look.

"I'd just die if I were locked in a room by myself," she finished in a calmer tone.

The feather had stopped completely, and now Isadora just sat staring at her. Under such an intense gaze, Camille waited to feel Isadora rooting through her brain, looking for information as if she'd lost something there.

"Any other education?" Isadora finally asked. "Besides homeschooling, I mean."

Camille faltered.

"Well, ah, Bettina has taught me reading, spelling, writing. A little bit of divination . . ." Camille trailed off.

Bettina doesn't have the patience to teach me, she almost said but stopped herself. The truth was that Bettina often became too exasperated to work with Camille, and left her to study by herself. In the end, distracted by the quiet, Camille would mostly day dream about exploring Chatham castle, sewing a new dress that wasn't linen or gray, or what it would be like to wear lacy gloves to tea.

"Is that all?"

"N-no. I've learned more," Camille said, eager to fill the silence but fearful that she'd somehow disappoint Isadora's expectations. Isadora gave an encouraging nod, acting as if she had all the time in the world.

Maybe she doesn't mind if I talk, Camille thought, the tension in her shoulders easing a little. *Bettina never wants me to talk.*

"Bettina is trying to teach me algebra," she admitted with a sheepish grin. "I'm terrible at it. Then she gets frustrated and tells me to figure it out and locks herself in her room for the rest of the day."

Isadora didn't seem surprised.

"What do you do then?"

"I try and figure out the Algebra," she said. "Really, I do! One day I worked on it for a full thirty minutes without day dreaming once. But I don't really understand math. Sometimes Leda helps me, but she's really busy studying too."

Isadora hummed something.

"Can you do transformations?"

"Not really, but I'd like to!" Camille leaned forward in her seat, a flush of excitement on her face. "Leda once transformed a white flower into a pink one. She doesn't really know how she did it, but it was so lovely! I'd love to change ugly gray rocks into a pretty rosebush, or something like that. Gardens are my favorite."

"Have you learned any of the ancient languages?"

"No." Camille shrugged. "I don't see the point. We only speak the common language in Hansham and most of the Central Network."

"How about divination?"

"Not really." Camille's eyes widened. "But that might be a fun thing to learn as well! Maybe it would help me make better decisions. Bettina says I'm terrible at making logical decisions."

"Logic doesn't always lead us down the right path," Isadora said, folding her veiny hands on her lap. "Tell me about Miss Kathy's. Mr. Hymas told me that you work in the bakery. Have you worked there for long?"

"Oh, yes!" Camille beamed. "I love working at Miss Kathy's bakery. I started a couple of years ago, at least. I had just moved here and was having a terrible time. I missed my parents so much. Miss Kathy knocked right on our door and said she needed help with deliveries. I wanted to get out of my aunts' stuffy house, and Bettina consented immediately."

Isadora's eyes narrowed almost imperceptibly. She paused for a moment with a thoughtful expression and then straightened up in her chair. The feather stopped writing.

"You seem to really love the bakery," she observed.

Camille put her hands to her flushed cheeks, eyes alight. "Oh yes! Miss Kathy named me her official sampler, you know. She let's me try a little taste of just about every batch of whatever she makes, but she won't let me work in the back yet. Says I'm not ready."

Isadora smiled and the feather laid down on top of the diary, which closed over it. Camille didn't notice.

"Why not?"

Camille let out another hefty sigh that tossed her bangs from her face. "I burned some cookies. Actually, I burned seven batches of cookies. But it was an accident!" she insisted. "I didn't know the oven got so hot!"

Isadora opened her mouth to speak but didn't have the chance.

"But she did say that I have a good sense of taste," Camille rushed to explain, lest Isadora think her incompetent. "Plus, I have a regular delivery route to some of the older people who live out in cottages and can't walk in every week. Everyone comes to the bakery. I think it's because of all the candy at the front. Most of the children like the sour candy best, but I like the lollipops. I know everyone in Hansham, you know."

Isadora smiled in an offhand way. "Yes, well, I think I've heard enough to make my decision," she announced.

Camille's stomach lurched, pulling her down from her happy world at the bakery and back to reality. "O-oh, yes," she stuttered, folding her suddenly cold hands in her lap. "Okay."

"I'm always completely honest with my applicants," Isadora said, looking Camille straight in the eye. "Academically, you are not a good choice based on what I can see in regards to your current level of education. Miss Mabel's is a very difficult school as far as the curriculum is concerned. There are many witches who simply can't keep up with the school work and expectations."

A cold feeling welled up in Camille's chest. It reminded her of the fear she first felt when she saw her parents lying in their graves.

"Your ability to concentrate is weak. As you said, you're prone to fits of daydreaming, emotion, and apathy. And there are many things at Miss Mabel's that you will not be interested in learning." A small smile came to Isadora's face. "Algebra included."

Camille looked down at her hands.

"You also rely on other people more than most, which dependency is not a trait of most girls at the school. I've seen it work out in a few cases, but most girls who attend Miss Mabel's are self-motivated, organized, and driven."

Bettina's words came back with haunting clarity.

Otherwise it'll be just your usual chaotic madness and you'll have no motivation.

Camille couldn't bear to look up, and could hardly endure the interminable stillness of the office in the meantime. She wondered how long she could keep it together, wondered how she would keep the scream in her throat.

Not long.

Of course Isadora was going to tell her that she wasn't what Miss Mabel's wanted. Why had she even hoped? She wasn't Leda or Fitz or Miss Kathy or Bettina. She was Camille, and that wasn't good enough. Isadora, seeing the look on her face, stopped and said, "Are you all right, Camille?"

Camille broke, crumbling into barely discernible cries.

"I hate Hansham!" she wailed, shame washing over her. "I hate the quiet house. I hate Bettina and Angie! I want to be with girls my own age. And even though Bettina says I should know, I don't know what I want to be! Maybe I'll be an apothecary so I can save people like my parents. Th-then little g-girls like me won't h-have to grow up an orphan with aunts that d-don't love her!"

The sobs wouldn't stop.

Camille's pent up craving for human touch, the overwhelming need for the comfort of a loving family, the hope of an escape from the austere grip of Bettina and Angie's house all bubbled up, flowing out of her in great hiccups and sobs.

Isadora waited patiently, her hands folded, her thumbs twiddling, for the emotional current to subside. As soon as Camille had let it all out, when her face was red and her nose dripping, Isadora floated a handkerchief over to Camille.

"Thank you," Camille mumbled, mopping her face and gazing up through her red, swollen eyes.

"Do you feel better?" Isadora asked.

Camille stopped to think it over.

"Yes," she said. "A little."

"I thought so. I'd like to invite you to Miss Mabel's School for Girls, Camille."

Camille's eyes shot up to meet hers.

"What?"

Isadora leaned back in her seat, but her twisted spine made it look like she was hunching forward.

"Welcome to Miss Mabel's School for Girls. You are invited to attend, if you would like to accept the offer."

Camille blinked, rendered speechless for the first time in her life.

"You're accepting me?"

"Yes."

"B-but why?"

"Because you belong."

"I can't belong there. I have so many weaknesses. You just told me all of them."

Isadora chuckled. "Yes, well, there's more to Miss Mabel's than that."

"Like what?"

"I'm accepting you for more reasons than your academic abilities, or lack thereof," she replied in an easy tone.

"So you're accepting me because you feel sorry for me?" Camille said, tears welling up in her eyes once more.

"No. I'm accepting you because you have an incredibly large heart, which is often a characteristic lacking at a school like Miss Mabel's. Your ability to love and be loved is much stronger than most witches', which is not at weakness at all. You belong at Miss Mabel's because you are more than just a student; you're a friend. And, from what I can see, you will be a very important friend to many people. You may not have found your purpose yet," Isadora allowed with a little twinkle in her eye, "but trust me when I say that you do have a path. Once you find it, it will be as clear as day."

A world of understanding seemed to pass between them in that moment.

Camille thought over what Isadora had said. Something was filling her, and she wasn't sure if it was relief or a new kind of fear—the kind of fear that came before she'd take on something much bigger and more frightening than she'd ever known before.

"Accepting the invitation to Miss Mabel's will mean a few things," Isadora said. "You'll be required to work hard over the summer to make sure you're caught up with the required education level, and you'll have to maintain that level of work ethic throughout your whole stay at Miss Mabel's. Learning doesn't come as easily for you as it does others, but with a lot of hard work, you can earn your marks."

Camille leapt to her feet with a happy cry.

"I accept!" she squealed. "Oh, Isadora, thank you. Thank you!"

Camille threw her arms around Isadora, a few more happy tears leaking onto her cheeks. Isadora patted her arm with a low chuckle.

"I'm so happy!" she said, and it flooded through every bone in her body. "So very happy!"

Priscilla

Priscilla studied the string of pearls with unnecessary scrutiny. Although their luster impressed her, the sheen coating the top layer couldn't have been natural. Another fraud. Incensed, she tossed them across her dresser with a careless flick of her wrist. The pearls hit with a clacking sound and slid to the end, where they dropped to the floor and rested in a heap.

"Poor excuse of a man," she muttered. "Even at fifteen I deserve better than fake pearls."

No, a little voice whispered inside her, sounding an awful lot like her mother. *Not unless you're perfect. If you were perfect, Mr. Rutherford's son would have bought you real pearls.*

Father had bought her real pearls the year he'd forgotten about her birthday, but the beauty of the necklace still hadn't swallowed the sting of his carelessness. It pinched her heart, even now. She never wanted to see another string of pearls—real or fake—again.

Priscilla's father, Jaxton, was the Coven leader for the prosperous city of Ashleigh, one of the wealthiest cities in the Central Network. He had worked hard to build and maintain that reputation, and Ashleigh delivered. Unfortunately, his job meant long hours away from home, running a city, and forgetting his family. It had been a week since they'd spoken. Priscilla brushed away the sudden pang in her stomach that meant she missed him. They'd been close, once.

"Doesn't matter," Priscilla said, shaking the voice off with a reminder of their wealth. "We can buy real pearls."

Not that she wanted them.

The smell of lilacs and candied almonds drifted towards her on the breeze. "At least I'm not a poor forester living in Letum Wood," she said with a petulant sigh. "Things could always be worse."

Sun streamed onto her face, warming her porcelain skin. For a moment she considered lingering there because it felt so good but instead stepped away from the light.

Tanned skin on a girl? Vulgar, Mother's voice whispered. *Your skin should look as white as snow.*

Priscilla folded her arms on the sill, keeping her head a safe distance from the sun, and gazed out at the ornate buildings surrounding their mansion. The elaborate iron fences, gardens fluffy with white, pink, and purple summerflowers, and sturdy oak trees with magnificent arms seemed to stretch out and embrace the city. A few witches walked by below, holding parasols over their heads. Their dresses, Priscilla noted, had fewer ruffles than last year's fashion. Something Mother had predicted.

"Blasted woman is always right," she muttered, envying the girls for their freedom. Escaping her bedroom and walking around Ashleigh would be a welcome reprieve from the monotony.

A complexion like yours can't handle the harsh sun, and we wouldn't want a blemish, would we? Mother's voice echoed like a bell in her mind with all the certainty in the world that a single flaw would bring about the collapse of Antebellum.

Not a single imperfection.

Priscilla rolled her eyes.

"Cilla, darling." A shrill voice called up the stairs, making her cringe. "Time for tea!"

She glanced over her shoulder. The closed wooden door was no barrier to a voice like Mother's. Steel couldn't stop something so high and demanding.

Priscilla walked over to a dress hanging from a padded hanger on a nail in the far wall. The crushed white velvet felt divine on her fingertips. Truth be told, a more ridiculous choice for tea didn't exist. The sleeves lacked the right lace and the extravagant figure wouldn't fit such a simple event. Mother would scorn it.

"But she insisted I find something memorable," she said out loud, as if the dress would answer back. It didn't, leaving her even less certain. Priscilla bit her bottom lip and looked at the other dresses crowding her closet. There were so many, yet none of them seemed right. As she pulled out a light pink one, her mother's voice played through her mind.

Pink is acceptable when you're ten, dear. But we must put on a more mature look for you now that you're fifteen and soon to be marriage material.

Stuffing it back into the closet with a huff, Priscilla eyed a light-yellow gown with an extra layer of lace around the top.

Too bright outside for yellow inside, Mother's voice chided in her mind. *You'd look like the sun, and one can't compare with the sun.* Frustrated, Priscilla dropped the dress to the floor of the closet, slammed the door closed with a crack, and gave a satisfied nod.

"I'll wear the white one," she said, "and Mother can deal with it. This is all Abigail's fault. If she didn't take so long doing her chores she could have already picked my dress out with Mother."

Blaming it on someone else eased the ball of anxiety in her chest.

If it's not good enough for Mother, Priscilla reasoned, *then it's because Abigail didn't come up after her lunch chores.*

She'd need help preparing for tea to Mother's satisfaction. Inevitably, there was always something she did wrong. Priscilla looked at the servant's cord on the wall and cast a spell. The cord bobbed up and down, as if pulled by an invisible hand. Why pull the rope when magic could do all the work? A tinkling bell sang in the servants' quarters far below, calling Abigail to her.

"Run, Abigail," Priscilla muttered. "Run as fast as you can."

It took several minutes, but eventually a light tap sounded on the door.

"Permission to enter, Miss Priscilla?"

"Granted."

Abigail moved into the room with all the presence of a mouse, eyes averted and shoulders hunched. *Good,* Priscilla thought. *She remembered not to make eye contact.*

"Prepare me for tea, Abigail. Mother has already called. We musn't be late."

"Yes, Miss Priscilla."

Abigail limped into the room, her lame right leg trailing a little behind the left. However much it hurt, she hid the pain. Grimacing was not attractive, even in a servant, which Mother reminded Abigail often.

"Bring my dress," Priscilla said, turning back to her mirror. Now that she'd completed her morning transformations, she could allow the servants inside. If they knew the truth, their gossiping little mouths would let all of Ashleigh know that the Mortons used transformative magic to look perfect. They'd be shunned and ridiculed, possibly ruining Papa's career.

The equivalent of the fires of hell in Mother's mind.

Secrets, secrets, Priscilla thought, wondering what it would feel like to let the truth go free. Would Mother burn with embarrassment? What would Priscilla do with her free time if she didn't have to practice more transformations? The appealing thought left as soon as it came.

Beauty is everything, Mother's voice reminded her.

Abigail appeared with the dress in hand, ready to slide over the see-through shift Priscilla'd been lounging in all day.

"Be careful!" Priscilla warned, nervous that a single out-of-place curl would draw Mother's attention. "I spent an hour on my hair. I'll not have you ruining my hard work."

Abigail bowed her head once but said nothing, as Priscilla preferred. They wrestled the dress over Priscilla's shoulders and down onto her curvaceous hips. Abigail pulled the silk ribbons up the back so that it tightened over Priscilla's chest, accenting her natural hourglass figure. She gazed down to see the top swells of her bosom.

You did come in a bit early, didn't you? Mother was right. Again.

"Cinch the waist a little tighter," she said, earning a silent nod of approval from her Mother inside. "I'm not sure who is here. I need to be ready for anything."

Abigail tightened and pulled the dress until it met Priscilla's satisfaction. Too small around the chest already, it pushed her breasts up like a pedestal. Breathing could be a problem, but that wasn't new. Priscilla stepped up to a gilded mirror and checked her reflection for any flaws. None, as usual. Not a single freckle on her alabaster skin. A little prickle of worry nagged at her anyway. Mother always found something.

"Would you like your new pearls?" Abigail asked, stooping to pick them up from the floor.

"No. They're fake."

Abigail's bushy eyebrows rose, but she wisely posed no question.

"Mr. Rutherford's son sent them over to me as a present for my birthday last week, but they aren't real. I can tell by the painted gloss on the outside. Really, Abigail," she drawled in a cruel tone, "don't you know anything about jewelry?"

The deliberate barb hit the mark. A quiet flinch on Abigail's face gave Priscilla a momentary feeling of power. Abigail wouldn't know anything about pearls—she'd been working for the Mortons since she could carry a tray. The closest Abigail would ever get to pearls was cleaning them.

"Get me the real pearls Father gave me for my birthday last year," Priscilla commanded. "The earrings as well. Mother will be upset if I don't wear the earrings. And hurry! She'll scold me for being late."

Abigail hobbled over to the armoire, where she struggled to reach the appropriate black box. The nuisance of her short height added to that of her gimpy leg made Abigail doubly handicapped. Priscilla watched, wondering if Abigail would let her practice a few transformation spells on her round, freckled face.

No, Mother would never allow it.

Many years before, just to throw the servants off, Mother had made Priscilla practice transformation on Abigail and fail on purpose.

Then there won't be the slightest suspicion, Mother had said. Priscilla did a spell that shredded Abigail's hair into short pieces and turned the ends purple. *An unfortunate accident,* Mother said, shaking her head back and forth while the servants bustled around them. *Priscilla won't be doing transformations anymore, will she?*

Abigail had worn a scarf around her head for months.

Priscilla shook her head, breaking off the memory. A little pang of remorse twisted her chest every time she thought of it.

Pretty is not beautiful, Mother's voice whispered through Priscilla's mind as she did a second check in the mirror. The ringlets still shone, perfectly coiled, resting on her shoulders. *And beautiful is never beautiful enough.*

"Abigail, who has come?" she asked to distract herself.

"I don't know who it was, miss. Just saw them briefly."

Once Abigail finally got hold of the case, she stumbled backwards, nearly falling over her leg and onto the bed. Priscilla shot her a sharp warning glare. Abigail recovered from the stumble, straightened, and brought the string of pearls in her reddened, chapped hands. Priscilla spun around to face her, red hair spiraling into the air.

"What did they look like?"

Perhaps it was old Mr. Rutherford's boring son, the one who couldn't even pick out the right kind of necklace. Boring, but an attractive distraction. Someone that her friend Stephany would enjoy.

"She was an old woman," Abigail said. "With two different-colored eyes."

"An old woman? Ugh. Maybe I don't want to wear pearls then." Priscilla batted them away. "My parents know far too many people. Forget the jewelry. I'm not out to impress an old biddy. Tidy up in here before you come down, Abigail. The blankets need airing."

Abigail bobbed an awkward curtsy. Priscilla disappeared into the hallway, her shoes lightly tapping on the hardwood floor as she walked.

Spine as a straight as a stick. Priscilla repeated her etiquette lessons in her head. *Walk carefully. If you're in the right mindset, you'll float.*

She descended the stairs one at a time to avoid the awkward hassle of not being able to breathe. Perhaps the bold style of this dress would offend whatever old woman had come. Then gossiping tongues would wag throughout Ashleigh and unravel all of Mother's hard work.

It sounded delightful.

Priscilla Morton wore the most scandalous dress to tea the other day, one of them would say, talking over their tepid tea and porcelain cups. *I don't know how I managed to get through the experience.*

"Too late to change now," she muttered to herself, feeling a shot of gratification.

A quiet exchange of voices stopped when Priscilla came into view. The wide staircase opened into the grand entryway, gilded with gold trim along the walls. She stepped off the last stair and onto the black and white tiled floor. Marble statues of previous Ashleigh coven leaders guarded the walls in stony silence, and candles sat unlit in their golden sconces. The austere elegance had a sharp feel to it, robbing the place of any homey warmth. Priscilla glanced to Mother, whose cool expression left no doubt that she found something wanting. The look quickly disappeared, replaced by Mother's usual beaming smile.

"There you are!" she said in the soft voice of a gentlewitch. "Priscilla, this is . . ." Mother trailed off, perplexed. She circled around to look at the old woman standing behind her. "I must apologize for my lacking manners. What did you say your name was again?"

The old woman smiled and stepped past Mother.

"I didn't. Merry meet, Priscilla."

Priscilla reluctantly took the proffered hand. The hag seemed like someone who had been attractive in her youth but had long since eroded into a mass of bone and wrinkle. Mother positioned herself just behind the visitor and gave Priscilla an arch look.

Be good or deal with me, it said.

"To what do we owe the pleasure of your visit?" Priscilla managed in a warm tone. It met approval, for Mother's eyebrow lowered. The woman smiled a toothy grin. Her yellow teeth jutted at awkward angles from reddened, swollen gums. Priscilla recoiled but hid it behind a cough.

"Excuse me," she said.

"I didn't come for much." The woman peered around the corner. "Do you have a warm fire? My hands are very cold, even on such a beautiful summer day. It's terrible getting old, you know. Not that you two would understand. You might as well be sisters!"

"Yes we have a fire," Mother said, simpering with the flattery. She sent Priscilla a frosty look over the woman's head. "You're welcome to sit there as long as you need."

Surely this woman wandered in off the road with an addled brain, Priscilla thought but kept her thoughts to herself. She'd rather visit with a total stranger than deal with Mother.

"Please," Priscilla said with the same sweet concern, extending her arm with a warm smile. "Come into our parlor."

Why she had to escort such a decrepit stranger to sit on their silky white furniture, Priscilla couldn't fathom. Mother wouldn't even let the servants sit on the furniture. Why would she let a smelly hag? The worn cloth of the old crone's dress would leave an eternal stain behind.

"Thank you," the visitor said, not relinquishing her grip on Priscilla's hand.

"Please," Priscilla said. "Have a seat."

Priscilla chose the mustard-colored chair, the darkest one in the room, but held little hope that it would remain clean. She brushed her hair over her shoulder with a careless wave. What did it matter? Abigail would clean it, not her.

"This is a lovely parlor," the old woman said, running her eyes over the large painting of Priscilla's grandfather positioned over the white mantle of the fireplace. It commanded attention and respect. Like all of her family, he had been a very handsome man, with a roguish smile and sparkling eyes. Priscilla imagined she would have liked him, had he lived long enough for her to remember. Flowers the color of sunshine decorated the mantle in white vases. In the middle was a quaint chandelier, which sparkled in the afternoon light.

"We like sitting in here," Priscilla said, catching a glimpse of her Mother watching from the hall. She turned away so the woman couldn't see her, and lowered herself into a seat near the stranger. "We sit here often with company. It's full of light, which makes for the best reading."

Keep up lively conversation, the internal voice of her Mother demanded. *One never knows when one is being assessed.*

"That's a lovely painting," the visitor said.

Priscilla's eyes flickered to the painting on the far wall. A bitter taste filled her mouth. Mother stared back at her, age fifteen. Her dark red hair, so deep it was more auburn than red, sat on her neck in an elegant coif, with tendrils fanning out around her. Her eyes seemed to laugh, and her lithe frame looked willowy and graceful.

"Yes," Priscilla said, unable to contain the edge that crept into her voice. "That's Mother when she was my age."

The expression on her face always made Priscilla shudder, like Mother could come back from the past and assess her still.

Clasped hands. Perfect hair. A smile without the teeth showing. Skin with no freckles.

"Her father had it painted for her birthday," Priscilla said, reciting the same story she'd heard for years. "She was perfection itself. Papa had a hard time getting her to agree to marry him because there were so many other witches in line to claim her honor."

"You bear a very strong resemblance."

The old woman's voice rolled in a musing way. Priscilla waved her hand and a nearby bell tinkled, requesting the maid to bring a tray of tea.

"Yes," Priscilla said. "So I've heard."

"It may be the green eyes. Or the flawless skin," the old lady said. "At any rate, I know many witches would love to have your looks."

Priscilla wanted to scoff. *They must not know how much work it is every day.* She gave a stiff smile in response, just as Mother had trained her.

"Thank you."

"Some witches would even use magic to transform their looks," the old lady said, with the intrigued look of someone pursuing an agenda. Priscilla stiffened. Her eyes flickered up to the old woman's face.

"I've heard rumors of that," she said carefully, her eyes narrowing.

The old woman chortled.

"Yes, we all have."

Priscilla didn't know what this meant, but she didn't like it. Her knuckles turned white, her hands blanched. An uncomfortable warning sensation crawled across her back.

"Magical transformation is more than a rumor," the visitor said. "It's a very real skill. A rare one when done right."

"Indeed," Priscilla whispered in a cold voice. "What did you say your name was?"

"I didn't. I came because you have a peculiar talent . . . or so I hear."

"Did you now?" Priscilla replied with a bit more cheek than necessary. The door into the parlor creaked just a little. Mother would be fuming behind it. Is this what Mother had wanted? Surely not. "And what talent would that be?"

The woman spread her lips into that same dank, toothy grin, unfazed by the snap in Priscilla's tone.

"Magical transformation, of course. You are a great beauty without the magic, but with it you're near perfect, aren't you?"

Near perfect. According to you and Mother, perfection is not absolute.

Priscilla looked away but didn't contradict her. How could the woman have known? This must be some kind of game Mother wanted to play. She decided to roll with it, to let it come about. The hag was not wrong. Her perfect figure and full, black eyelashes were no accident. Neither were Mother's full head of hair and stunning profile.

"I was wondering if you would be able to share your gift with me," the old woman continued. "Perhaps demonstrate your talent on an old hag like me."

"Absolutely not." Priscilla stood up, her face flushing a bright red color. "I don't allow strangers to come in off the street and beg me to make them beautiful."

Priscilla turned away. The demented woman tipped her head back and laughed.

"Who said anything about being beautiful? All I want is to smooth out a few wrinkles, or at least make this hair a little fuller. Think of it as a present for an old woman."

Priscilla hesitated and looked to the doorway. Mother mouthed the words *do it* with thin lips and an irate expression. Priscilla's stomach turned cold.

"Why do you want to be different than you are now?" she asked, looking back to the old woman. "Why aren't you good enough?"

The old woman stared at her for a long moment, probing, assessing. Priscilla held her breath, wondering why this moment felt so important.

"Personal reasons," the woman finally said and left it at that. Priscilla lifted her eyes back to the doorway, taking in Mother's calculating expression.

Nothing is good enough. Never, never enough.

"Are you sure you want this?" Priscilla asked, hesitating. She'd never done it on anyone besides Mother and herself. Perhaps the magic wouldn't work on someone so old, or when she felt so much pressure, or without any practice. Magic worked best with familiarity, on faces she already knew. Suppose she made the woman look worse? Mother would likely entertain thoughts of kicking her out of the house.

That wouldn't be so bad.

"Just a touch up," the woman said. "I don't entertain any hope of looking like you by the end of it."

Priscilla drew in a deep breath, forcing herself to relax. She imaged the skin on the woman's face smoother, the bags under her eyes erased, the hair long and full. She closed her eyes and put the magic into motion by whispering the right incantations under her breath.

At first the magic fought. Her aged body, little more than skin and knotted bones, resisted the change. Priscilla struggled to keep focused on the right incantation, keeping them even and consistent, the picture in her mind clear.

The process took several minutes. Slowly, the wrinkled planes of the old woman's face tightened. Her eyelids lifted so that they didn't droop quite as far. What few tendrils of hair that peeked out from her hood lengthened, spilling onto the black cape around her neck in coils of silver. Her eyes brightened, shedding their dim light to sparkle and shine.

It's gratifying to have so much talent and skill, Priscilla thought, casting a critical eye over her work. *Perhaps I could find a career path in transformation and break away from Mother's rigid fist.*

"And does that meet your satisfaction?" she asked with a haughty lift of her eyebrow.

The old woman beckoned towards a small mirror nearby, conveniently resting on the sideboard. She gazed into the mirror for only a second before standing up.

"Yes, it does."

A scroll appeared in her hand, replacing the mirror. A premonition crept up Priscilla's back in a cool chill. This couldn't be just any old woman. Mother appeared in the doorway.

"Tea is here!" she cried, an exultant, flushed look on her perfect cheeks.

The old woman began to change. All the wrinkles Priscilla had fixed returned. The teeth didn't yellow again, but they didn't sparkle anymore. The woman's hair shortened, forming into a loose bun at the back instead of the nearly-bald tendrils of before.

"What did you do?" Priscilla cried. "You changed my work!"

"I did," the old woman said. "I'm not a hag by any means, but neither do I enjoy caring for long hair. This is an invitation to join Miss Mabel's School for Girls." The scroll in her hands lifted into the air and hovered just within reach of Priscilla's fingers. "You passed my interview."

"Your interview?"

"Yes."

Miss Mabel's.

The name alone sent her body into nervous flutters, like birds flying underneath her skin. That meant the old woman was Isadora, the famous and powerful Watcher. She had just been sassy to one of the most powerful witches in the Central Network. Priscilla stared at the scroll with a feeling of disbelief. Isadora's thin lips lifted into a smile, as if she had read Priscilla's mind.

"Your transformation skills are very strong, as your mother said in the application she made on your behalf. They lived up to my expectation and then some. You'd do well with transformation as a career. I'm also giving you a chance at the school because you did exactly what I asked you. Too many girls do more than they are asked in a bid to impress me. We could use more students who do as they are told."

"Yes," Priscilla muttered. "Who wants to work with students who are willing to do more than their superiors ask of them?"

"Priscilla!" Mother said with a sharp tone, her nostrils flaring. Priscilla clutched the scroll in a tight fist. It was all so embarrassing. She'd read this wrong from the beginning. Isadora simply smiled.

"In a world of unexperienced magical teenagers, no one."

"I thought you interviewed people," Priscilla said, meeting Isadora's eyes although she didn't want to. She felt betrayed and angry.

"I do."

"But you didn't ask me any questions."

"The best part of an interview rarely does," Isadora said. "Let me caution you on pride. You have a great deal of it, and that's far too much. You'll not last long in a school like Miss Mabel's if you indulge in it overmuch. Also be aware that your insecurities run your mind. You can't let that continue forever, or it may turn you into someone you don't want to be."

Isadora's eyes flickered to Mother and back again. Priscilla's back tightened, receiving the silent message.

"Merry part, Priscilla," she said, then turned and faced her mother. "Jeannette."

Without another word, Isadora smiled, then walked to the door and let herself out. Priscilla and her mother stood there for several seconds, stunned. Then Priscilla ran to the window and looked out, but no signs of Isadora remained.

"Well, that was quite a surprise," Mother said in a breathless voice. "I can't wait to tell the ladies at tea later today! What do you think? They'll just die from jealousy, I think. You'll need to change that dress of course. It's not proper. What were you thinking? Oh, and I think we should try and curb the attitude in future exchanges, hmm?"

The windowpane in front of Priscilla fogged up beneath her breath.

You'd do well with transformation as a career.

"Yes, Mother," Priscilla said, wondering if she'd just inadvertently been handed her freedom.

Michelle

The soup foamed and frothed.

Perfect, thought Michelle, pulling in a deep breath. It smelled like salty broth, sweet carrots, and the lightest hint of basil. *The scent is just right. Maybe a pinch more salt. I'm glad I found those dried herbs.*

"You have to keep stirring, Mace," she said. "Or else the chicken will burn to the bottom. See?"

The six-year-old standing beside her rose to his tiptoes and peered over the brim of the pot. The scent of winter and bay leaves drifted through the house. A few chopped carrots swirled in the aftermath of the moving spoon, stirred from the dregs at the bottom.

"I see. Can I ask you a question, Meesh?"

"Sure."

"Why do I have to sing the soup song?"

"Because it helps the soup cook better. Just like the bread song makes bread fluffy, and the pie song makes pie sweeter. It's part of the magic."

Mace thought for a second, his eyebrows pulling together.

"Papa doesn't like it when you use magic to cook," he said. "He says food tastes fine on its own."

Michelle handed him the spoon and ruffled his thick brown hair.

"Yes, well, Papa eats the food anyway, doesn't he? Here, you take over. I'm going to go get some more firewood. You don't have to sing if you don't want to."

Mace took the spoon and started to sing a song about dragons under his breath. It wasn't the soup song, but he seemed pleased with it. Michelle chuckled softly, swung a knitted shawl over her shoulders, and plunged into the winter snowscape outside. The fading light meant that each minute the world grew colder. Against a freeze this piercing, her homemade shawl was no more protection than a coat of butterfly wings.

The wind slid past in an arctic blast, whipping the lazy snowflakes into whirls about her waist. Blankets of snow piled up against the trees at the far end of the yard. Letum Wood looked especially dark and menacing against the snow.

Shivering, Michelle stepped onto the packed trail that forked in three different directions. One to the barn, one to the well, and one to the lean-to where the firewood waited.

The cold bit the end of her nose. She lifted a hand to cover it and promptly lost her balance on a patch of ice, falling into the nearest snowbank with a poof. She muttered under her breath in frustration, pushed off the fluffy pile, and continued on.

The lean-to door creaked when she pulled it open. Rust covered the nails, tearing them away bit by bit in the constant exposure. *I feel like that sometimes,* Michelle thought. *Useful, but stuck.* She shook her unfaithful thoughts away. The shanty might get boring in the winter at times, and the scenery never changed, but at least she had a warm bed. Many of the farmers and foresters out here didn't have even that, not in this forsaken, quiet part of Letum Wood on the southern edge of the Network. The village a couple miles away didn't even have a name it was so small.

Her billowing breath obscured the view of the firewood as she stood there, trying to figure out the best place to start. They needed a big log to bank for the night and smaller pieces to keep it warm. Moving quickly, Michelle grabbed as many logs as could fit in her arms, which was a substantial number for a girl, and turned to go. Like her father, she was built strong and thick, able to carry as much as her older brother Blain.

By the time she made it back into the log house, Mace was stirring the pot with a gusto that had slopped soup over the sides and dribbled it close to the fire. With every wave of soup he made a crashing sound.

"Mace!" she scolded. "You're wasting food."

Although the door had slammed against the wall when she entered, Mace jumped at the sound of her voice anyway, too absorbed in his song to have heard her approach. A blush crept across his cheeks.

"Sorry, Meesh."

The sweet tone of Mace calling her by the old family nickname stopped her annoyance. She could never stay frustrated with him for long.

"Just be careful," she said and dropped the logs by the fire. They continued working in silence as Michelle pulled a loaf of bread from the old stove and grabbed a pat of butter to smear it with. The edges of the crust had turned a dusky brown, and the middle sank in.

"I can never get it right," she muttered in frustration.

Mace took a break from stirring to stoke the fire. The back door flew open, admitting a troop of four burly, towering men.

"You're early!" Mace cried, jumping off the stool. "Why are you back so soon?"

Ted, the oldest, spoke first.

"Too cold to cut. The ice is forming around the tree trunks. We can barely even stand without falling."

Taking the hint, Michelle grabbed a few logs from the stack, built up the fire, and then pushed the chairs from the table around the flames. With everyone home, the cabin filled with life and bodies and a surprising quiet. Michelle continued her duties without a word. As the men began to thaw out, their talk increased, but never rose above an easy, steady hum. That's what Michelle liked about home. It was quiet, even when it was loud.

By the time her brothers had taken off their thick coats and hung them on the pegs by the back door, Mace had peered into the pot and looked back to Michelle.

"Is it ready?"

"I think so."

Mace gave it another stir and announced, "It's ready." Then shot Michelle another look to make sure he was right. She nodded once. "It's ready!" he repeated, this time with his usual dramatic gusto, and flung himself off the stool again, headed towards his older brothers, who began tossing him around.

The four men stood up, shuffling around the table already set with bowls and spoons. They were a troop of giants—at least, that's what the other foresters called them, even though the foresters that lived and worked in the wintry bowels of southern Letum Wood were historically a brawny people. Michelle lifted the heavy pot, hefting it over to the table, and setting it in the middle. Her father nodded his approval.

"Smells good."

Her brothers mumbled a response. Mace brought over the imperfect loaf of bread, set it next to the dish of butter, and settled beside Ted. Once Michelle sat down, dinner began.

"Did you get enough firewood?" Michelle asked, halfway through the silent meal. Her father nodded once.

"Found a new hunting place," Rian, the third oldest, just above Michelle, said. "We're going to try it out tomorrow."

"There wasn't anything in the traps," James reported, flicking a glance towards his sister, in answer to the question on the tip of her tongue. "I'll get you some meat after we look at the new place."

Another silence followed. The slices of bread disappeared one at a time. Michelle helped herself to a second bowl of stew and was halfway through her first bite when Papa cleared his throat and spoke up.

"Got a letter today."

When the quiet grew awkward, Michelle looked up from her bowl and realized that Papa had addressed his comment to her. She lifted her eyebrows in question, but Papa wasn't looking at her anymore. Instead, he was scraping his wooden bowl. His black whiskers moved up and down when he spoke again.

"It's from your teacher. Seems she thinks you should go to a Network school instead of the school in town."

Michelle felt as if a stunning spell had smacked her dead in the face, rendering her body useless. Her breath stalled in her chest like a dying wind. She didn't know what to say.

"A-a Network school?" she finally managed.

"It's called Miss Mabel's. I've heard of it before. Your mama mentioned it a few times when you were a little girl."

The mention of her mother seemed to bring another blow. Her brothers gazed down into their bowls. Papa only mentioned her when it couldn't be avoided.

"What would I learn?"

"You could learn magic better than any of us have." He sat back in his chair and motioned to her brothers with a wave of his hand. "We get along without knowing as much because we do physical labor. Don't need magic to swing an ax."

"Some do," Blain muttered bitterly into a piece of bread. Many foresters held contempt for the witches in the wealthy northern cities of the Network. The lazy attitude of the northern witches was a usual complaint at the family dinner table. Michelle tensed, waiting for Papa's usual tirade on the over-dependence most witches placed on magic. He said it made them weak and pathetic. This was part of the reason that everyone in her family was built tall and strong, like a group of oxen.

"You want me to learn more magic?" she asked, gaping. Ted and Mace both looked up now, equally surprised. "You don't believe in magic."

"I believe in magic," he said, bristling. "I don't believe in using it to be slothful. You could learn it as a trade and not be lazy about it."

"But Papa, I don't want—"

"Besides, you're a real good cook, and you like doing it." His tone made it clear she didn't have a choice. Michelle felt her heart shrivel a little inside. He couldn't make her do this. Surely, he wouldn't.

Wouldn't he? her heart whispered. Yes, he would. Once Papa got an idea in his head, he followed it through.

"You could learn some kind of cooking specialty, I'm sure. Maybe work for the High Priestess."

Michelle put her hands in her lap, overwhelmed. It was true. She did love to cook. It was the only place she didn't feel awkward, clumsy, or too big for the space given. The spices, the herbs, combining them together in just the right quantities was all second-nature. Mama had taught her all the cooking songs to use before she died, songs that had been in her family for generations. The music was the magic of cooking, creating different emphases on flavors and textures. Cooking made sense to Michelle. It brought her comfort. And there was always someone to cook for, always a sense of being needed.

But to work for the High Priestess? That wasn't what she wanted to do. At least, not really. It would be fun to see a castle, to learn more about cooking the perfect loaf of bread. She didn't want to leave her brothers or her home to do that, though. Besides, they didn't need her at Chatham Castle. Her family needed her here. So why was Papa doing this?

"Did I do something wrong?" she asked in a small voice.

For just a moment, Papa's beady eyes softened from beneath his heavy brow. He let out a gruff breath and the room shifted into an awkward pause. Papa cast his eyes around and set down his spoon.

"No, Meesh. You didn't do anything wrong."

Ted drained the last dregs from his cup before setting it down. "Papa promised Mama before she died that he'd send you some-where so that you could make a name for yourself," he said, meeting Michelle's inquiring gaze. "She didn't want you stuck in this house forever, taking care of us."

Michelle wanted to cry, but she couldn't. The tears didn't come. Not since Mama died. Not since she saw the blank, stricken look of fear on Papa's face when Ted and Rian finished filling Mama's grave. No, Mama's death made it impossible to show any weakness. Papa needed their strength.

"You have to interview with Isadora, the Watcher. She's coming by tomorrow."

"Tomorrow?" Michelle cried, her head snapping up. Papa stood, his chair scraping across the wooden floor.

"Yes, tomorrow," he said in a firm tone. There would be no more questions, no more discussions. "I'm going to take care of the cows. Mace, Rian, Blain, you come with me. James, see that the goats and chickens are taken care of."

Michelle didn't notice her family dispersing, nor the concerned looks Mace sent her way. She stared at the grain of the wood in the ta-ble until the lines merged. Only Ted remained behind. Stubble shadowed his face, his strong jaw highlighted by the same thick neck Papa had. Ted had light hair like Mama, with dark wisps of color near the roots. He was the oldest, and the one Michelle trusted most.

"Do you want to go, Meesh?" he asked.

She jumped, yanked from her thoughts by the sound of his voice but wouldn't meet his gaze.

"No," she whispered. "There would be so many other girls there. I-I . . . They already make fun of me at school as it is!"

The village schoolroom was over an hour's walk through the thick winter drifts, which meant she only made it once or twice a month. Because of all the time she had during the day, Michelle always kept up with, if not surpassed, the studies of the other students. The cabin grew lonely and close after awhile, but was still preferable to the snickers and laughter of her peers.

"If I go to a Network school, they'll tease me," she said. "They'll call me a poor forester!"

Ted leaned forward, his dark, intense eyes boring into her.

"You can't be afraid of things you don't know or understand. Believe it or not, you're the lucky one, Michelle. The rest of us didn't get a chance to learn magic the way you can, not after Mama died. It's too late for us now. We're strapped to a life of physical labor with some magic in between to help us get by. But you can do something different."

Was he crazy? She would have to leave home, live in a school surrounded by strangers. There would be tests, classes, and lessons she didn't understand. Even if she never did magic again, she'd rather stay at home, cooking for her brothers for the rest of her life.

But then, she realized with a sinking feeling, *that must be the point.* That was why Papa was sending her. Michelle would stay here, taking care of the boys, and never leave. That would be all she'd ever do. A little corner of her heart whispered, *It would be so fun to learn, to see something besides these walls.* She turned the voice away in mute frustration.

Ted waited for her response with a patience that reminded her of Mama. She'd been dead for years, since Mace was born, but so much of her lived here still.

"I don't want to go," she said.

"I know. But you'll learn to love it."

Ted gave her a small, crooked smile, rose from his chair, pulled on a hat and disappeared into the inky night. Left in the quiet of the house, Michelle started collecting the dishes with a methodical movement and sinking them into the bucket, watching them bubble and submerge in the hot water until she felt as if she'd drown in it herself.

White cotton puffs of fresh snow decorated the trees early the next morning, blown in by the overnight blizzard Michelle had stayed awake listening to. The sun was up, but a vague patch of gray and white covered the sky, sprinkling ice on the world. This morning, Letum Wood held a bitter chill.

Several pieces of wood toppled out of her arms and into the snow when Michelle heard a voice behind her. She lumbered about, nearly tripping over her feet, to see an aged woman standing a few paces away.

"Merry meet," the stranger called.

The old woman's breath frosted out in a fog when she spoke. Michelle put a hand to her chest to stop her heart from beating right out of her ribcage.

"Merry meet," she mumbled. "Can I help you?"

"Yes, you can," the old woman said. "We can go inside and finish this interview so I can get back home in time for tea. I don't really like the snow."

Michelle's eyes widened.

"The Watcher?" she asked in a breathless gasp.

"Yes. Let's go."

Isadora turned around and headed for the poor shanty, whose door opened to admit her before she arrived. Michelle stood, rooted to the spot.

I'm not ready for this!

She'd woken up hoping the entire conversation over dinner had been a dream, a vague nightmare. No one had spoken over breakfast, not a word, so Michelle had tucked the fear away. A dream, yes. That was all.

"Are you coming?" Isadora asked, turning to look for her. Michelle scrambled to gather up the sticks, but her nervous, fumbling hands managed to corral only about half of them. She abandoned the rest and joined Isadora.

"Very nice," Isadora said, looking around the trim house. The shabby, worn shanty smelled sweet, like burning pine. A hand-sewn quilt was draped over a rocking chair near the fire, and cast iron skillets hung from wall. The table, though wobbly, was large and sturdy, the centerpiece of the home. The bedrooms hid upstairs, with Michelle's little room separated from the rest. "You take very good care of this house for a girl so young."

Michelle averted her eyes.

"Thank you," she said, kneeling at the fireplace to stack the logs. A chilly draft blew in, and Michelle realized that she'd left the door open. Flustered under Isadora's watchful gaze, Michelle headed back towards the door with the logs still in hand, but they tumbled and fell to the ground in the middle of the dirt floor.

"S-s-sorry," she mumbled, pausing again, unsure as to whether she should shut the door or regather the firewood first. "One moment, please."

Isadora moved towards the fire, her curved back looking like the S-shape of a snake as she shuffled forward.

"No rush. The fire is nice."

Michelle finally got the door closed, cleaned up the wood, and took her time carefully stacking the logs by the fire. Isadora hummed quietly while she waited. Hands shaking, Michelle wiped her palms off on her apron.

"You can have a seat," she mumbled.

"I'm sorry dear, what did you say?"

Michelle motioned towards the table with her large paw-like hand.

"You can have a seat."

They sat across from each other. The hefty chair, carved by Papa's own talented hands, dwarfed Isadora. Her feet dangled an inch or two above the floor. Michelle stared fixedly at the groove lines in the table, making a mental note to scrub it down with the bristle-brush later. When she did sneak a glance up, her eyes met the hazy gaze of the old woman, and she looked right back down.

"What do you do to keep yourself busy during the day?" Isadora asked.

"School work," Michelle said. "And clean the house. I teach Mace. Or cook."

Another long silence.

"Do you ever wish you had a grandmother figure in your life?"

Michelle looked up at the strange question, but Isadora didn't seem to notice.

"A grandmother?"

"Yes."

Michelle shrugged. "I don't know."

"You prefer baking over cooking, don't you?"

"Yes."

"And you sew your own clothes."

"Yes. I sew my brothers' clothes too."

Isadora's forehead narrowed. "Hmm. They seem to rely on you for a lot of things."

"They do!" Michelle said eagerly, grateful that Isadora saw it her way. "I shouldn't leave them."

Isadora's eyes narrowed.

"Have you ever thought of making more friends?"

Michelle hesitated, knowing she couldn't lie and say "no." Sometimes, when the house got really quiet, or her thick fingers hurt from sewing, or she had no one to talk to, Michelle longed for a friend. Living in their little shanty often grew isolating, especially with Mama gone.

"Maybe." Michelle looked away again. "The girls in the village are . . . they don't like—they're busy."

Isadora made a humming noise in her throat.

"Well, despite that, you seem very happy here," Isadora said.

"I am," Michelle said too quickly, looking up through her bangs. Isadora lifted an eyebrow in interest.

"Can you tell me why?"

"Why I'm happy?"

Isadora nodded.

Michelle took a minute to ponder that, which soon stretched into an awkward silence. She stammered through her reply.

"M-m-my brothers."

"Is that the only reason?" Isadora asked with a meaningful gaze.

"No," Michelle whispered, looking back to the table. The fire crackled in the silence, waiting for her to speak. Her throat tightened up. She didn't want to say it.

"I know that Miss Mabel's is not your first choice for your future," Isadora said gently, when Michelle remained quiet. "I'd like you to tell me why."

Michelle hesitated, feeling exposed and vulnerable, like Mama had died all over again. She wanted to bluster her way through it, avoid the question, but one look at Isadora told her that the old woman wouldn't let that happen.

"It's safe here," Michelle finally admitted.

"Is it?"

"We're far from the village, from the people who live there." Michelle's thoughts flickered to the cutting remarks of the girls at school. *What are you? A giant? Look at Michelle, she's got hands the size of platters!* "And the strangers that walk through," she added on, as if that added to the danger of the sleepy village. "We're safe out here."

"Or you think you are."

Michelle's eyes snapped up to her again. Her thick forehead ruffled.

"What do you mean?"

"Your mother died in a sudden, tragic accident with a runaway horse and carriage just after your youngest brother was born. Now you're afraid that something you can't anticipate will happen to you, or your family."

There was no question in Isadora's statement, so Michelle couldn't duck away from it. Is this what Isadora did to every student? It felt like sticking her hand into a cauldron of lye, or putting out a fire by walking on it barefoot. Panic, hot and restless, shot through Michelle. She jumped to her feet. Her awkward frame bumped the table and sent her chair flying back, toppling over. She stumbled, feeling frazzled and trapped.

"I'm not afraid!" she cried, even though she knew it was a lie.

"We all are," Isadora said in an easy tone. "Even your strong father and brothers. It's a part of life, a part of being a witch. Fear isn't the problem. Not acting because of fear is."

"I don't want to go to Miss Mabel's!" Michelle cried, her hands clenching into fists. "I want to stay here!"

Isadora stared at her for a long time. She didn't stand up, didn't move. Then she quietly said,

"I have a good feeling about you, Michelle. What if I can guarantee that nothing will happen to you while I'm there?"

"You can't promise that."

"Yes I can. I'm the Watcher."

Isadora's calm, even tones settled the uneasy burn in Michelle's chest, scaling it back to a just-bearable amount. Michelle studied her, bold for the first time.

"What about my family?" she demanded. "You can't keep them safe."

"No. I can only guarantee your safety."

Michelle thought back to the firm resolve in Papa's eyes over dinner. The sadness, the regret. He felt as if he'd failed her, raising her in a house of men, part boy herself. She thought of making friends, of learning more about cooking than what she could here. Her cakes always fell. Her bread burned on the outside and went uncooked on the inside.

If she went, it would be for Papa. To keep him from feeling guilty. Then, once she'd learned more magic, she could come back and help them, teach them, like Ted said. They had taught her a few magical spells, mostly things they did to play pranks on each other, like deception spells. She knew they'd want to learn more.

"Can I come home during the summer?" she asked. Isadora smiled.

"Yes, you can."

Michelle swallowed the terrified ball in her throat. She didn't want to do this. She didn't want to start over at a new school, to meet girls that would surely make fun of her. But she'd do it for Papa, for her family.

"I'll do it," she said, lifting her terrified eyes to meet Isadora's. "I'll go to Miss Mabel's."

Isadora smiled and leaned back with a satisfied sigh.

"I think that's a very wise decision. Yes, very wise indeed."

Made in the USA
San Bernardino, CA
13 May 2015

21275204R00040